S0-ARY-270

How Is Peanut Butter Made?

by Grace Hansen

abdopublishing.com

Published by Abdo Kids, a division of ABDO, P.O. Box 398166, Minneapolis, Minnesota 55439.

Copyright © 2018 by Abdo Consulting Group, Inc. International copyrights reserved in all countries. No part of this book may be reproduced in any form without written permission from the publisher.

Printed in the United States of America, North Mankato, Minnesota.

052017

092017

THIS BOOK CONTAINS RECYCLED MATERIALS

Photo Credits: Alamy, Glow Images, iStock, Shutterstock

Production Contributors: Teddy Borth, Jennie Forsberg, Grace Hansen

Design Contributors: Dorothy Toth, Laura Mitchell

Publisher's Cataloging in Publication Data

Names: Hansen, Grace, author.

Title: How is peanut butter made? / by Grace Hansen.

Description: Minneapolis, Minnesota : Abdo Kids, 2018 | Series: How is it made? |
    Includes bibliographical references and index.

Identifiers: LCCN 2016962400 | ISBN 9781532100475 (lib. bdg.) |
    ISBN 9781532101168 (ebook) | ISBN 9781532101717 (Read-to-me ebook)

Subjects: LCSH: Peanut butter--Juvenile literature. | Peanut butter processing--
    Juvenile literature.

Classification: DDC 664/.726--dc23

LC record available at http://lccn.loc.gov/2016962400

Table of Contents

Peanut Farms

Peanut seeds are planted around April. Peanut plants are ready to be **harvested** in September or October!

5

Farmers gather the plants. The peanut plants sit in the sun for a few days. This dries them. Then the peanuts are separated from the vine.

Shelling

The peanuts are sent to a shelling plant. Their shells are removed. The peanuts are packed into big bags.

The Factory

The bags of peanuts are sent to a peanut butter factory. Stems, sticks, and other things are separated from the peanuts.

11

The peanuts are put into a **roaster**. Then they are cooled.

The peanuts then head to the **blanching** machine. Here, the skin is separated from each peanut. The peanuts are split in half. The **hearts** are removed.

15

The peanuts are cleaned
one last time. Smooth peanut
butters are made in grinders.
Chunky peanut butters are
put through choppers.

Salt and other ingredients can be added. But many peanut butters are made from 100% peanuts!

19

Ready For PB&J Sandwiches!

The peanut butter is poured into jars. The jars are sealed and labeled. Then they are ready to be shipped to stores!

More Facts

- Around 540 peanuts are in a 12-ounce (355 mL) jar of peanut butter.

- United States presidents Thomas Jefferson and Jimmy Carter were peanut farmers.

- Creamy peanut butter is more popular on the East Coast of the United States. Chunky peanut butter is more popular on the West Coast.

Glossary

blanch – to remove the skins of nuts by making them very hot for a short period of time.

harvest – the gathering of ripe crops.

heart – also called a nub, the heart is the embryo of a peanut. An embryo is found inside all seeds.

roaster – a device for browning and drying peanuts.

23

Index

abdokids.com

Use this code to log on to abdokids.com and access crafts, games, videos and more!

Abdo Kids Code:
HHK0475